We Gather Together...
Now Please Get Lost!

Diane deGroat

SeaStar Books
NEW YORK

Copyright © 2001 by Diane deGroat

All rights reserved. No part of this book may be reproduced or utilized in any form or by any means,
electronic or mechanical, including photocopying, recording, or any information storage and retrieval system,
without permission in writing from the publisher.

SEASTAR BOOKS
A division of NORTH-SOUTH BOOKS INC.

First published in the United States by SeaStar Books, a division of North-South Books Inc., New York.
Published simultaneously in Canada, Australia, and New Zealand by North-South Books,
an imprint of Nord-Süd Verlag AG, Gossau Zürich, Switzerland.
Library of Congress Cataloging-in-Publication Data is available.

The artwork for this book was prepared by using watercolors.
The text for this book is set in 14-point Korinna.

ISBN 1-58717-095-7 (trade binding)
1 3 5 7 9 TB 10 8 6 4 2
ISBN 1-58717-096-5 (library binding)
1 3 5 7 9 LB 10 8 6 4 2

Printed in Singapore by Tien Wah Press

For more information about our books, and the authors and artists who create them, visit our web site: www.northsouth.com

To Andrea Spooner,
who saw that no author, illustrator, or any form
of poultry was harmed in the making of this book.

Gilbert was so excited that he tossed and turned all night. Tomorrow his class was going on a field trip to Pilgrim Town, and Gilbert kept thinking about how much fun it would be. Frank was going to be his buddy for the trip, and promised to bring his checkers for the bus ride.

Gilbert *finally* drifted off to sleep when. . .

BAM!

Something bopped him on the head. Gilbert woke with a start and fell off the bed. His sister Lola laughed and waved her doll around. "You have to get up," she said.

"I *am* up," Gilbert said. But he was really down on the floor, stuck between the bed and the wall.

Lola tried to bop him again. "Mom says you're late for school!"

Gilbert had never been late for school, but today he was tired and didn't want to get up.

When Gilbert stomped into the kitchen, his socks didn't match, toothpaste was dribbling down his shirt, and his hair was sticking up in all the wrong places.

"Oh dear," Mother said when she saw him. "It looks like you got up on the wrong side of the bed today!"

She handed him his lunch bag as he hurried out the door. Gilbert had missed breakfast, and his stomach growled all the way to school.

When he got to his classroom, Mrs. Byrd had already marked him absent. She erased the "X" next to his name and said, "You should be thankful that we didn't leave without you, Gilbert!"

Gilbert wasn't so thankful when he saw that everyone had already picked their partners for the trip. The only person left without a buddy was Philip.

Philip was always the last one to get picked for anything. He couldn't catch a ball or run fast. He was also a big tattle-tale. And now he was Gilbert's buddy.

When the bus started down the road, Gilbert looked around. Frank and Kenny were playing checkers. Patty and Margaret played Travel Battleship. Lewis and Sam read a comic book. Gilbert and Philip just sat.

Gilbert's stomach growled again. He opened up his lunch bag, but Philip said, "I'm telling the teacher that you're eating on the bus."

Gilbert closed the bag.

Finally Mrs. Byrd said, "Now, class, we're almost there. At Pilgrim Town we'll see how the early settlers lived. They were thankful that they got through a hard winter, and celebrated their first harvest with a Thanksgiving feast. During our visit today I want you to think about all the things that you can be thankful for."

Patty raised her hand and said, "I'm thankful that no one threw up on the bus."

Lewis shouted, "I'm thankful that we didn't have to do spelling today." Everyone laughed. Except Mrs. Byrd—and Philip, who was the best speller in the class.

Gilbert just slouched in his seat and said, "I'm thankful that we're almost there."

When the bus pulled into the parking lot, Mrs. Byrd said, "Remember to stay with your buddy at all times so no one will get lost."

Two by two they walked through the village, where people in costumes talked about how the pilgrims lived. As they headed toward the blacksmith's shop, Gilbert ran to catch up with Frank and Kenny. Philip ran after him, calling, "Hey, wait for me!"

Frank said, "Too bad we can't be triple buddies, Gilbert.

But you have to stay with Philip."

When Philip caught up, he said, "Don't walk so fast, Gilbert. Mrs. Byrd wants us to stick together."

So Gilbert walked really, really slowly. Philip pulled at his sleeve, and said, "Hurry up, Gilbert."

At the hay barn, Gilbert hid behind a group of older kids, but Philip found him. "Stop it, Gilbert," he whined. "I'm telling Mrs. Byrd that you're fooling around."

"You're a big tattle-tale," Gilbert said. "Why don't you just get lost!"

"I'm telling Mrs. Byrd that you called me a tattle-tale," Philip said.

On the way to the picnic area Gilbert slipped into the restroom when Philip wasn't looking, and locked the door behind him. Now Philip would never find him!

picnic area

Gilbert waited a few minutes, then went to unlock the door. The lock wouldn't turn.

He tried again, but it was stuck.

He banged on the door, yelling, "Hey, Philip! I'm in here!"

Philip didn't answer.

Gilbert banged on the door again. "Is anyone out there?" he shouted.

No one answered.

Uh-oh, Gilbert thought. If Philip didn't see him go into the bathroom, no one would know he was in there.

Or worse—Philip might not even tell anyone that Gilbert was missing. That's what Gilbert would do if he were Philip. The class might leave without him, and Gilbert would have to spend the whole night there. Alone . . . in the bathroom . . . in the dark!

Suddenly the doorknob jiggled. "Is somebody there?" Gilbert shouted.

It was Philip. "Gilbert!" he said. "I've been looking all over for you."

"I can't get out!" Gilbert said. "The lock's stuck!"

"Hold on," Philip said. "I'll get help."

After a few minutes a guide came with the key. When Gilbert finally got out he saw Philip, but not the rest of his class. "Uh-oh," he cried. "We lost our class!"

The guide smiled and said, "Then we'd better check the lost and found."

As they walked to the visitors' center, Gilbert knew he was going to be in big trouble. And Philip was too—all because of him.

Gilbert waited anxiously with Philip at the Lost Child Corner until the class appeared. But Mrs. Byrd wasn't mad. She said, "There you are! I'm so glad we found you!"

Lewis wasn't so glad. He said, "We could have been eating lunch already, but we had to come looking for you and Philip."

Gilbert said, "It's not Philip's fault. I was hiding from him and got locked in the restroom. But he found me and got help."

Patty said, "Oh, Gilbert. You weren't being a very good buddy."

And Frank said, "I'm glad Gilbert wasn't *my* buddy."

But Mrs. Byrd said, "Let's just be happy that we are all safely here together." To celebrate, she bought some pies and pilgrim hats and led the class outside to a picnic table.

When they were all seated, she said, "Tomorrow is Thanksgiving Day. What are some of the things we should be thankful for?"

"Pumpkin pie!" Lewis said, helping himself to a piece. "Thanks for getting lost, Gilbert!"

Patty said, "I'm thankful that we don't have to live like the pilgrims did. They didn't have TV."

"Or comic books," Sam added.

They went around the table. When it was Gilbert's turn,
he thought for a minute, then said, "I'm thankful that I didn't have
to spend Thanksgiving locked in a bathroom. Thanks, Philip."

Everyone shouted, "Yay, Philip!"

Philip turned red, and said, "That's what buddies are for."

On the walk back to the bus Gilbert stayed close to Philip. Very close. On the bus Gilbert borrowed Frank's checkers, and he and Philip played five games.

Philip won every time.

Happy Thanksgiving!